To The Kids at Brooklyn Elementary,

Happy Reading!

Ruth Irene Garrett

4-27-10

Ruthie Goes to Town

Stories of a little Amish girl

Ruth Irene Garrett

Illustrated by Rhonda Mullins Dellepiane

STEWARD & WISE PUBLISHING
Morley, Missouri

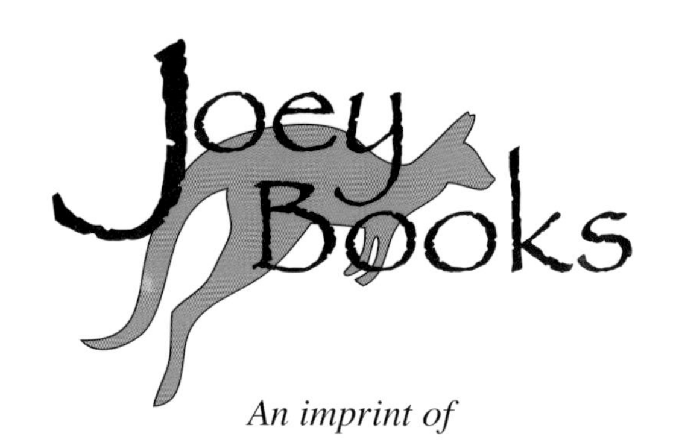

An imprint of

STEWARD & WISE PUBLISHING
Your Next Great Book
P.O. Box 238
Morley, MO 63767
(573) 262-2121

Publishing Consultant: Douglas W. Sikes
Book Designer: Elizabeth B. Sikes
Cover Designer: Emily K. Sikes

Illustrator: Rhonda Mullins Dellepiane

Artwork Scanning by Glenda Westrich and Floyd Evans
Cape Blueprint, Cape Girardeau, MO

Library of Congress Control No.: 2005936532
ISBN: 0-9773198-2-2

First Printing: 2005 A.D.
Printed in the United States of America
10 9 8 7 6 5 4 3 2 1

Contact us at **www.stewardandwisepublishing.com**

Visit Ruth at **ruthirenegarrett.com**

Dedication

This book is dedicated to my husband's oldest daughter Julia Meyers, her husband Ross, and their children Carmen and Sean.

Acknowledgments

As with most books, it takes many friends and family to make it work. With that said, I would like to thank my husband Ottie for helping to create *Ruthie* and for drawing the storyboard. I had a vision of *Ruthie,* and Ottie was able to convey graphically what I could only imagine. I am grateful to Rhonda Mullins Dellepiane, our illustrator, for her beautiful art work. Thanks to Barry and Christina Jones and their children Robbie and Collin; Jeff and Tammy Pedigo and their children Brook, Morgan and Zebulan; Stan and Pat Birchem and their grandchildren; and to our wonderful new publisher and editors at Steward and Wise, and the Doug Sikes family for all the wonderful things they have done to help create the *Little Ruthie Series* and actualize this dream.

Ruth Irene Garrett

This book belongs to Ruthie's new friend,

____

Given by

____

Little Ruthie Series

Ruthie Goes to Town

This is a story about a little girl named Ruthie Miller, her family, and her little dog Heidi. They live in America, probably not far from where you live.

Ruthie is Amish, which means her family still lives

and farms as people did more than a hundred years ago. Amish do not use electricity, have telephones or cars like the rest of us do today, and they speak a different language at home called Pennsylvania Deutch. But you will see she's still very much like you.

As the sun began to rise, the Miller Family woke up to a new day. It was time to start the morning chores.

Suddenly Ruthie's puppy Heidi jumped up on her bed and started licking her face.

"Stop it, Heidi, I'm awake!" Ruthie giggled.

The whole family gathered in the barn to milk the cows, the first chore of every day. Everyone shares in the work on an Amish farm. Father, or as Ruthie called him, *Dat,* milked the first cow. Ruthie held the cow's tail so that it couldn't hit Dat as she swished it at the flies. Kitty licked up a bowl of warm milk as Heidi played with the kittens.

After the milking, the family gathered for breakfast. Everyone bowed their head as Dat said a prayer. As breakfast began, Ruthie slipped Heidi a delicious piece of bacon. Heidi wagged her tail in

delight. Dat put down his cup and announced, "Children, when the rest of the chores are done, we are going to town today!"

Ruthie could barely contain her excitement.

After breakfast, Ruthie helped her *Maem,* feed the chickens and ducks, her *very* favorite chore. Heidi barked at a hen and the hen clucked back huffily. Billy the pony waited patiently to be fed.

Heidi
watched
curiously as
Ruthie and her big
sister Carmen pumped water
for the chickens in the hen house.

Pumping is hard work, and Ruthie is not strong enough to do it by herself.

Her two brothers Phillip and Sean helped Dat with the other chores to get everything done quickly.

All the children were very excited since they only get to go to town together once or twice a year.

The boys helped Dat hitch Lucy the horse to the buggy and they set off to town. This is the way an Amish family travels when they go somewhere. On the way, they met their neighbors, Saloma Schrock and her daughter Faith. "Hello!" the Millers exclaimed, waving to their friends.

For their first stop in town, Dat wanted to make a quick visit to Mr. Jones' feed store. He let Ruthie go with him, but he told the rest of the family to wait in the buggy. As they entered the store, Mr. Jones' two boys stared curiously at Ruthie.

While Dat was
busy talking to Mr. Jones,
Mrs. Jones said, “Ruthie would
you like some gumdrops?”

JONES
FEED STORE

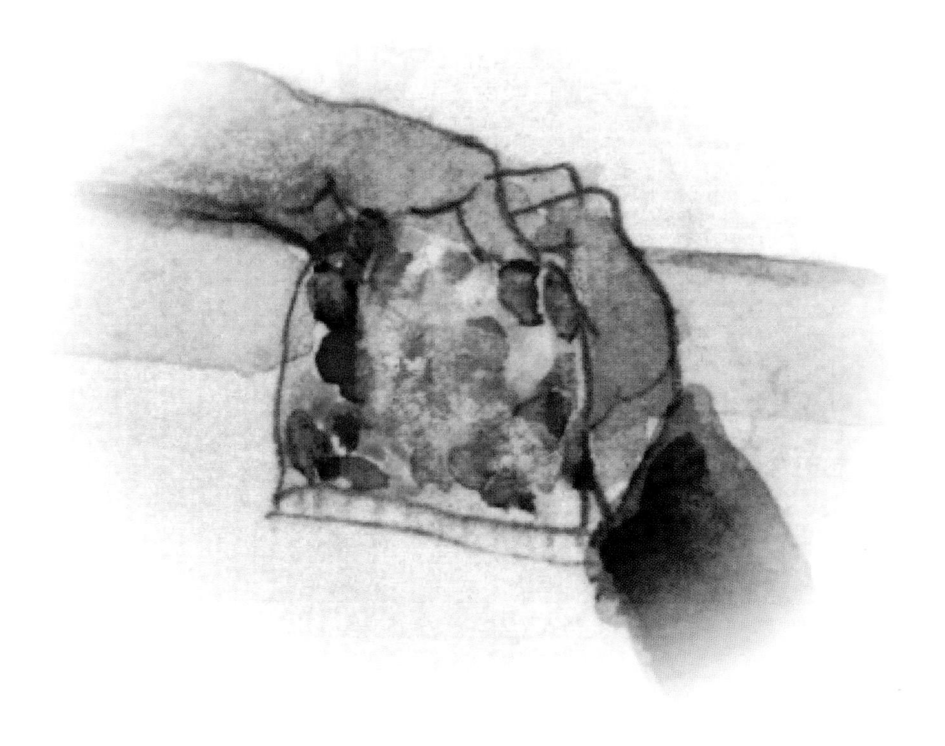

Since Ruthie didn't know many words in English, she timidly nodded her head "Yes." Mrs. Jones pulled out a small bag of colorful gumdrops. Ruthie had never seen so much yummy candy before. Almost too excited to speak clearly, she finally managed to say, "Th-thank you!"

Ruthie admired the beautiful bag in her hand. "How many are in there?" she wondered. "Oh look, there are six red ones, my *favorite* color!" She thought about Carmen, Phillip and Sean and slowly slipped the bag into her dress pocket hidden under her apron.

After leaving the feed store, Maem wanted to stop at Yoder's Variety Store. She needed material to make new Sunday clothes for the family. Ruthie and Carmen chose the colors they wanted for their new dresses while Dat and her brothers were looking at shop tools. Ruthie said, "I want mine to be *red!"* Carmen exclaimed, "Not me, I want blue for mine." Maem said, "I think blue will do nicely for both of you."

They all climbed into the buggy to go home, but Dat had a surprise. “We’re going to Pedigo’s for an ice cream cone!” he announced. Ruthie knew just what she wanted, *strawberry*. Soon, Bishop Birchem and his wife arrived to buy some too. A bishop is the leader of an Amish community. “So good to see all of you,” declared Bishop Birchem. Sean waved through the window at some other customers while Dat talked to the Bishop. Then it was time to go home.

edigo's
Sodas
Fries
Hamburgers

As the buggy pulled into the driveway, Heidi and the farm dog, Ellie, came running to greet them. Heidi barked happily as Ruthie called to her, “Heidi... I’m home!”

Ruthie could tell that Heidi missed her while she was in town. Heidi was very excited that she was back, and ran along beside her as Ruthie skipped down the path to the garden.

Carmen followed Ruthie to the garden, carrying a basket. "Maem said for us to gather vegetables for supper." Ruthie picked the red, juicy tomatoes and Heidi chased a hungry little rabbit out of the garden. In the barn, Dat and the boys began the evening chores.

FRESH
SWEETCORN
NO SUNDAY SALES

They heard a car pull up in the driveway. It was their neighbor Rhonda and her three children. They were not Amish, but stopped in quite often to buy vegetables, eggs, and milk. Rhonda visited with Maem for a few minutes as Ruthie put the ears of corn into a bag. Heidi made Ruthie giggle as she wrestled with an ear of corn, eager to help.

Ruthie still had the bag of gumdrops in her pocket. "What should I do with it?" She wondered. She went to her room, hid the candy under her pillow, and got her doll, Martha. Heidi followed Ruthie to her secret spot in the garden. Ruthie asked Heidi and Martha, "What should I do? The candy *was* given to me...oh, I would like to keep it all for myself, but Carmen, Phillip, and Sean like candy just as much as I do. I don't want to be selfish." Heidi licked Ruthie's hand and barked as if to say, "Do what you know is right." After a few minutes, Ruthie's face brightened with a smile, and she said to Heidi, "I have an idea, but for now this is our secret!"

That evening everyone helped with the milking again. While Maem and Phillip milked the last cow, Sean and Ruthie gathered up the milking stools to put them away. Dat said, "Carmen, please help me carry this milk to the ice box." Suddenly they heard Heidi yip. She found a little black mouse hidden under a pile of hay!

Ruthie thought that her family would never finish eating their supper. Finally, everyone's plate was empty and Maem was about to clear the table. Ruthie couldn't wait any longer and burst out, "I have a surprise!" Everyone looked at Ruthie. "Mrs. Jones gave me a bag of gumdrops. I really wanted to keep them all for myself, but that made me feel bad. So I decided to share them with all of you!" Ruthie beamed as she saw their happy faces when she gave each of them some candy.

After supper Dat sat down to read the paper. Maem worked on her sewing while the children wrestled with Heidi. Carmen, Phillip, and Sean thanked Ruthie for sharing her candy with them. Ruthie smiled. She was happy that she had done the right thing.

At bed time, Heidi joined Ruthie at the window as she knelt to say her prayers. Ruthie gazed at the starry sky and began.

"Thank you, God, for my family and for helping me to share." Ruthie smiled at Heidi and said, "It feels so good to make others happy, and the candy tasted much better too!"

As a silvery full moon rose over Miller Farm, Ruthie drifted off to sleep, cuddled up with Heidi in her soft feather bed. Both dreamed of another day with more adventures and surprises on their Amish farm.

About the Author

Ruth Irene (Miller) Garrett grew up Amish on a farm in Kalona, Iowa. She is now a best-selling author with three previous books on Amish life, including her most recent biography, *Born Amish*. She resides with her husband, Ottie Garrett, Jr., in Glasgow, Kentucky. She lectures frequently on Amish life to eager audiences across the country, and has been featured in numerous magazines such as *Glamour* and *Marie Claire* and television broadcasts such as *20/20*.

About the Illustrator

Rhonda Mullins Dellepiane is an artist, living in Denver, Colorado, with her husband and three children. *Ruthie goes to Town*, the first in the Little Ruthie Series, is the fourth book she has illustrated. The others include *Goodbye, Geraldine*, a novel by Robert J. Morgan, as well as two textbooks, *Dinner Time* and *Our Book of Dua*. She has been working as an illustrator, graphic and mixed media artist for 17 years. You may contact her at RhondaArt@aol.com. Rhonda dedicates this book to her grandmother and mentor, Beth Lehman.